**LOCK UP YOUR BOYFRIENDS,
GIRLS OF BEAR COUNTRY.
BERMUDA McBEAR
HAS COME TO TOWN!**

It's only natural for a shy guy like Brother to have a crush on a good-looking older girl like Bermuda. But there's something odd about the way she has come after him.

Sort of like a shark attacking its prey.

Has Bermuda chosen Brother because she really likes him? Or is there another reason?

BIG CHAPTER BOOKS

The Berenstain Bears and the Drug Free Zone
The Berenstain Bears and the New Girl in Town
The Berenstain Bears Gotta Dance!
The Berenstain Bears and the Nerdy Nephew
The Berenstain Bears Accept No Substitutes
The Berenstain Bears and the Female Fullback
The Berenstain Bears and the Red-Handed Thief
The Berenstain Bears
    and the Wheelchair Commando
The Berenstain Bears and the School Scandal Sheet
The Berenstain Bears and the Galloping Ghost
The Berenstain Bears at Camp Crush
The Berenstain Bears and the Giddy Grandma
The Berenstain Bears and the Dress Code
The Berenstain Bears' Media Madness
The Berenstain Bears in the Freaky Funhouse
The Berenstain Bears
    and the Showdown at Chainsaw Gap
The Berenstain Bears at the Teen Rock Cafe
The Berenstain Bears in Maniac Mansion
The Berenstain Bears and the Bermuda Triangle
The Berenstain Bears
    and the Ghost of the Auto Graveyard

The Berenstain Bears and the BERMUDA TRIANGLE

by the Berenstains

A BIG CHAPTER BOOK™

Random House New York

http://www.randomhouse.com/

Library of Congress Cataloging-in-Publication Data
Berenstain, Stan.
The Berenstain Bears and the Bermuda Triangle /
Stan and Jan Berenstain.
    p. cm. — (Big chapter books)
SUMMARY: Brother Bear has a crush on an attractive older girl
at school, but his friends are suspicious when she comes after him
in an aggressive manner.
ISBN 0-679-87649-9 (pbk.). — ISBN 0-679-97649-3 (lib. bdg.)
[1. Behavior—Fiction.   2. Bears—Fiction.   3. Schools—Fiction.
4. Mystery and detective stories.]   I. Berenstain, Jan.
II. Title.   III. Series: Berenstain, Stan.   Big chapter book.
PZ7.B4483Bebc   1997
[Fic]—dc20
96-25935

Printed in the United States of America   10 9 8 7 6 5 4 3 2 1

Contents

1. Bonnie's Rude Awakening   1
2. The Invisible Green-Eyed Monster   7
3. Queenie's Theory   11
4. Rejected Again   16
5. A Change of Heart   22
6. A Heart of Change   26
7. Brother in Trouble?   33
8. News from the Gossip Queen   37
9. Let's Do Lunch   45
10. Triangles   48
11. Bonnie Makes Her Case   53
12. Tailing the Suspect   60
13. "Elementary, My Dear Lizzy"   65
14. Bonnie's Bag of Tricks   71
15. Hacking for a Good Cause   80
16. Bermuda's Confession   92
17. Crime and Punishment   99

Chapter 1
Bonnie's Rude Awakening

Brother Bear and Bonnie Brown had long ago stopped being an "item" at Bear Country School. When they had first gotten together during a school performance of Shakesbear's *Romeo and Juliet,* everyone had expected them to become boyfriend and girlfriend. But as things turned out, there was more friendship than romance between them.

Brother and Bonnie liked each other, and they liked the same things. Bonnie sometimes did professional acting in plays and TV commercials, and Brother liked acting, too. They were both interested in nature and science, and they both liked reading mystery stories. They often went to the movies together. At school they always sat together at lunch. And every day they walked home together from school.

But even though Brother and Bonnie were mainly good friends, there was just enough romantic feeling between them to make Brother jealous whenever Bonnie paid a lot of attention to another guy. That happened from time to time, because Bonnie was cute and bright and fun to talk to. Quite a few guys wanted her attention. And Bonnie was also a friendly cub who wouldn't ignore a guy just because Brother got a little jealous. After all, she and Brother weren't really boyfriend and girl-friend.

Brother was a popular cub, too, and girls

liked him. But he was shy. What's more, girls knew that Bonnie liked him. They all wanted to be Bonnie's friend, so they were careful not to make her jealous of them. Once in a while, Queenie McBear would flirt with Brother for a minute or two. But Bonnie knew that Queenie flirted with *all* the guys—mostly to make Too-Tall Grizzly jealous. So Bonnie wasn't jealous of Queenie. In fact, Bonnie had never been jealous of anyone.

Then, one fall day, Bonnie's whole world changed.

It was lunchtime at Bear Country School.

Brother had paid for his lunch and taken his tray to the usual table. Bonnie was next in line. She paid for her lunch, too, then started to walk to Brother's table. She had gone just a few short steps when something made her stop and stare.

Brother was talking to an older girl cub. Bonnie had first noticed this cub only a few days earlier in the schoolyard. She remembered her because of her flashy, eye-catching clothes. And she was dressed the same way now. She wore a shiny purple headband, gold hoop earrings, a bangle necklace, a designer top, and a purple miniskirt over bright red stretch pants.

But it wasn't just the new cub's clothes that caught Bonnie's eye. It was her behavior, too. She was sitting right beside Brother, leaning toward him. Actually, leaning *into* him was more like it! And she was

looking into his eyes as if he were the most interesting cub she'd ever met.

Brother was looking back at the older cub as if *she* were the *cutest* cub he'd ever laid eyes on. Definitely not the *most interesting* cub he'd ever met, thought Bonnie, because Brother seemed to be doing all the talking. But he was talking to her as if she made him feel like the most interesting cub in all Bear Country.

"What's the matter, Bonnie? Forget something?"

It was Cousin Fred bringing his tray from the lunch line. He always sat with Bonnie and Brother. Now he saw what Bonnie was staring at. "Hmm," he said. "We'd better go join them. Right away..."

Bonnie was feeling something she'd never felt before. *Jealousy*. It embarrassed her, and she didn't want Fred to notice. So she said, "We shouldn't just barge into their conversation, Fred. Let's give them some privacy. We can sit with Babs and Queenie instead."

Fred shrugged. "Okay," he said. "If you say so."

Chapter 2
The Invisible
Green-Eyed Monster

Babs Bruno and Queenie McBear looked up in surprise as Bonnie and Fred sat down at their table.

"And what, pray tell, do we owe this great honor to?" Queenie teased.

"What's wrong?" said Bonnie. "Don't you want us to sit with you?"

"Sure we do," said Queenie. "I'm just wondering why you aren't sitting with Brother—you know, like you do *every other* day."

Bonnie took a sip of her milk and tried to look calm. "Brother's...busy," she said.

Queenie and Babs looked over at Brother's table. Babs gasped. Queenie chuckled.

"I guess it was just a matter of time," said Queenie. "That girl is trouble."

"Who is she?" asked Babs.

"Bermuda McBear," said Queenie.

"McBear?" said Fred. "Like you?"

"She's my cousin," said Queenie. "My aunt and uncle want to move to Beartown, but they haven't been able to sell their house in Big Bear City yet. So they sent Bermuda to live with us in the meantime. That way she can get adjusted to Bear Country School while the school year is still young. Now, *I* think she's more interested in getting adjusted to Beartown boys than Bear Country School. So you'd better

lock up your boyfriends, girls."

"She certainly doesn't seem shy," said Fred.

"Shy?" said Queenie. "Compared to Bermuda, *I'm* shy."

"She looks older than us," said Babs.

"She's a year ahead," said Queenie. "She's in Teacher Harriet's class. The boys in *that* class don't stand a chance. Their grades are gonna drop right through the floor!"

Bonnie took another sip of milk and swallowed hard. She had a huge lump in her throat. She looked down at her tuna sandwich. Suddenly she felt sick to her stomach. "Excuse me," she mumbled. Then she got up and hurried out of the lunchroom.

The cubs stared after her.

"Wow," said Fred. "Why'd she do that?"

"Something chased her out," said Queenie. She took a big bite of her tuna sandwich and chewed it hungrily.

"I didn't see anything chasing her," said Fred.

"Of course not," said Queenie, still chewing. "It was the Invisible Green-Eyed Monster."

Chapter 3
Queenie's Theory

Cousin Fred looked puzzled for a moment. "Invisible Green-Eyed Monster?" he said. "Oh, I get it. You mean she's jealous."

"Bingo," said Queenie.

"But that doesn't make sense," said Fred. "Bonnie's never acted jealous before."

Queenie and Babs looked at each other and rolled their eyes.

"Boy, oh boy," said Queenie, shaking her head. "What guys know about romance could be written on the head of a pin."

"What do you mean?" said Fred.

"Let me ask you a question," said Queenie. "What planet have you been living on?"

"Something tells me this isn't an astronomy quiz. But I'll play along," said Fred. "Earth."

"Well, in all your time here on planet Earth," said Queenie, "have you ever seen a girl go after Brother the way Bermuda's going after him right now?"

Fred thought for a moment. "No," he said. "Can't say that I have."

"There's your answer," said Queenie.

Fred looked puzzled. "What was the question?" he asked.

Queenie sighed. "The question was: Why haven't you ever seen Bonnie act jealous before?"

Fred thought hard again. When it came to math, science, and the dictionary, which he read for fun, Fred's mind was as nimble as a circus acrobat. But with boy-girl stuff it was a different story.

Finally, a light blinked on in some long-forgotten corner of Fred's mind. "I got it!" he said. "You're saying that Bonnie has never had a good reason to be jealous before. Right?"

"Right, Bearlock Holmes," Queenie sneered.

Just then, Ferdy Factual and Trudy Brunowitz sat down at the table. Ferdy and Trudy were a couple in the same way that Brother and Bonnie were a couple: more just friends than boyfriend and girlfriend. But, like Brother and Bonnie, they had just enough romantic feeling toward each other to cause problems with jealousy now and then.

"Bearlock Holmes, the great detective?" said Ferdy. "Why are you discussing him?"

"We're not discussing him," said Babs. "Queenie was just making fun of Fred." She repeated Queenie's theory about why Bonnie had never acted jealous before.

"Very logical," agreed Ferdy in a bored tone of voice. "But we cannot test your theory until Bonnie is given a proper opportunity to be jealous."

"You came a couple minutes too late," said Babs. "Bonnie just had her first encounter with the Green-Eyed Monster."

"And what did she do?" asked Ferdy. He yawned to make it seem as if he weren't really interested, but the look in his eyes gave him away.

"She jumped up and ran out of the room," said Queenie.

Ferdy yawned again. "But how can we be sure it was jealousy that made her behave in this manner?" he asked. "How do we know it wasn't something else? A bad tuna sandwich, for example?"

"For one thing, Mr. Science, she never took a bite of her tuna sandwich," said Queenie. "For another, look over there."

Ferdy and Trudy looked in the direction Queenie was pointing. Their eyes grew wide. Bermuda now had a hand on Brother's arm. Her face was so close to his that she was almost kissing him.

"Hmm," said Ferdy. "Something tells me Brother hasn't had a bite of *his* tuna sandwich yet, either."

Trudy moved her chair closer to Ferdy's, as if to guard him from the new girl. "Something tells *me* Brother wouldn't care if he missed lunch altogether," she said. "Maybe dinner and dessert, too."

Chapter 4
Rejected Again

Later that day, when the bell rang for afternoon recess, it looked as if Bonnie and Brother had already patched things up. They were about to walk out to recess together when Queenie hurried over to them and said, "Hey, wait up, guys."

Now, Queenie usually walked out to recess with the Too-Tall gang. So Bonnie knew right away that there was just one thing on Queenie's mind: *gossip.* Queenie must have seen Brother and Bonnie whispering to each other while Teacher Bob was writing on the blackboard. And now she wanted to be the first to know what all the whispering was about so she could spread the news around the schoolyard.

Bonnie's suspicion turned out to be right on target. As the three cubs walked down the hallway toward the side entrance, Queenie leaned over to Bonnie and whispered, "Well, what did he say?"

"Shhh," Bonnie whispered back. "Later."

But there was no stopping Queenie when she smelled a juicy piece of gossip. She kept nudging Bonnie, until Bonnie finally had to tell Brother, "You go on ahead. I'll catch up with you."

Brother took off, and Bonnie hung back with Queenie. By now Babs had joined them.

"Well, what did he say?" asked Queenie.

"What part of *later* didn't you understand?" said Bonnie.

"I want to know, too," urged Babs. "I'm

worried about you and Brother."

"Me too," said Sister Bear, who had just hurried over with Lizzy Bruin. "I saw what happened in the lunchroom."

"There!" said Queenie. "This is Brother's own sister speaking! She has a *right* to know!"

They started walking slowly down the hall, as other cubs eager for recess streamed around them.

"Oh, all right," said Bonnie. "I asked Brother why he was being so friendly to Bermuda. He said it was just because she's new in town. He wants to make her feel welcome."

"Is that all?" said Sister.

"That's what he says," said Bonnie.

"And do you buy that?" asked Queenie.

"I'm willing to give him the benefit of the doubt," said Bonnie.

"Oh, is that so?" said Queenie. "Well, *I'm* willing to *doubt* there's going to be any *benefit* in being a wimp about it."

Bonnie glared at Queenie. "Why are you trying to cause trouble between Brother and me?" she demanded.

"*I'm* not trying to cause trouble!" said Queenie. "*Bermuda's* trying to cause trouble!"

"Maybe she is," Bonnie admitted. "But that doesn't mean Brother is going to let her. As a matter of fact, he just promised to show me some of his soccer moves at recess. I bet he's waiting for me right outside the entrance."

But when the cubs reached the side entrance, Brother wasn't there. They

scanned the schoolyard for him.

"There he is," said Sister, pointing. "He's out on the soccer field. Uh-oh…"

That one little phrase—*uh-oh*—plucked Bonnie's heartstrings. And it made them go *twang*. She looked out at the soccer field and saw Brother bouncing a ball from knee to knee as Bermuda McBear beamed at him.

Bonnie's face fell. She felt a sudden stabbing pain in her heart.

"Come on," said Sister. "Let's go break it up."

"No, thanks," muttered Bonnie. "I'm going back inside. I just remembered… uh…Teacher Bob asked me to…er…help him with something during recess." She turned and hurried back down the hall.

"That's terrible!" said Babs. "Second time today it's happened! Brother ought to be ashamed of himself!"

"Look at him!" said Queenie. "He ought to change his name from Brother Bear to Brother *Dog*."

"Huh?" said Lizzy.

"He's acting just like a little puppy dog," said Queenie. "You can almost see him wag his tail whenever Bermuda looks at him. I bet he'd roll over and play dead if she told him to."

Chapter 5
A Change of Heart

Usually Bonnie walked home from school with Brother, Sister, and Cousin Fred. But when the final bell rang that afternoon, she flung her backpack over her shoulder, dashed out of Teacher Bob's classroom, and headed quickly down the hall without her friends.

Bonnie figured that Sister and Fred were going to wait for Brother, who hadn't gotten back yet from performing his duties as principal's aide of the month. During the last period of each day, Brother had to make his rounds, walking from classroom to classroom to make sure the blackboard erasers had been cleaned and the suggestion boxes had been emptied. He also had to check the supply room to see if everything was in order. It was a big responsibility for a cub, and Brother took it very seriously—so seriously, in fact, that sometimes he didn't finish until a minute or two after the final bell. When that happened, Sister, Fred, and Bonnie would wait for him in the hall outside Teacher Bob's classroom.

But this time Bonnie had no desire to wait for Brother. Just the opposite. She was still angry about being ignored at recess and lunch. Angry *and* jealous. And that was a combination that made her feet move faster than ever. She strode down the hall so swiftly that she reached the front entrance

before any other cubs had left their class-
rooms.

When she got to the bottom of the front
steps, though, something made her stop.
She stared at the empty schoolyard and the
cars going by on the road beyond the fence.
She realized that she had never been the
first cub out of school before. She was all
alone. It felt weird. And kind of lonely.

Bonnie turned and looked back at the
entrance. She began to think. Maybe she
was being a bit silly. Jumping to conclu-
sions. Did she really have a good reason *not*
to believe Brother about why he was being
friendly to Bermuda? After all, he *was* the
principal's aide that month. Maybe he felt a
responsibility to welcome new students and

make them feel at home. And, now that she thought about it, Brother hadn't really ignored her today, either. It was *she* who had decided not to sit with Brother at lunch, wasn't it? And wasn't it also she who had hung back with Queenie in the hallway at recess? Hadn't she told Brother she'd catch up with him? Then why had she been angry when he didn't wait for her outside the entrance?

Bonnie decided to wait for Brother, Sister, and Fred. A nice calm walk home with Brother might be just the way to show him she wasn't angry anymore.

Besides, she thought, *even if I were still angry, that wouldn't give me the right to be rude to my other friends.*

Bonnie heaved a sigh of relief. She felt better already.

SEE YA, GUYS.
BYE, BONNIE!

Chapter 6
A Heart of Change

Quite a few cubs had come down the steps
and passed Bonnie before Sister and Fred
finally appeared in the entrance. But
Brother wasn't with them. Instead, Queenie, Babs, Lizzy, Ferdy, and Trudy were.
They looked as if they'd just been discussing something important in the hall.

Now they saw Bonnie standing at the
bottom of the steps, and their expressions
changed instantly—from serious to embarrassed. Ferdy and Trudy hurried down
the steps. "See ya, guys," they called back.

"Bye, Bonnie!" Bonnie noticed that Trudy had Ferdy's arm in a vise-like grip.

Then came Babs and Queenie. "Call me later if you want to talk," Queenie told Bonnie as she hurried off with Babs.

Finally, Sister, Lizzy, and Fred came down the steps.

"What's going on?" asked Bonnie. "Hasn't Brother gotten back from his rounds yet?"

"Uh…no," said Fred. "I mean…he's tied up…we'd better not wait for him. Let's go…"

Just then Brother appeared in the entrance. And he wasn't alone. With him was none other than Bermuda McBear. And they were *holding hands!*

Bonnie felt that queasy feeling again in the pit of her stomach. Part of her wanted to turn and walk off toward home without looking back. But another part wanted to stand there and stare at the two lovebirds. And it was the second part that won.

Brother and Bermuda were so busy talking to each other that neither of them noticed the cubs until they reached the bottom of the steps.

"Well, *hello* there," said Bermuda to Fred. "You're kind of cute."

Fred instantly turned several shades of red. A goofy grin spread across his face.

"Uh...hi, guys," said Brother. "This is Bermuda McBear, Queenie's cousin."

"We know," said Sister, glaring at Brother.

"Bermuda, this is my little sister," said Brother. "And this is Cousin Fred. And this is...er...uh...Bonnie Brown."

If there had been a rock nearby, Bonnie would have crawled under it right then and there. Brother had almost forgotten her name!

Bermuda giggled and smiled at Bonnie. Bonnie had a jealous look on her face, and Bermuda seemed to be enjoying it.

Bermuda put a hand on her hip and winked at Fred. "I'm in Teacher Harriet's class," she said. "Do you know where that is?"

"Uh, sure," said Fred. "Right up the hall from mine."

"Then you should come up and see me sometime," crooned Bermuda.

Fred's face was now the color of a beet. "Sure," he said. "I..." But Sister elbowed him in the ribs before he could finish his sentence. "Ow! I mean...I'm kind of busy this week..." Sister elbowed him again. "Ow! I mean this month. Ow! This *year!*"

Bermuda threw her head back and laughed. "I was just kidding, nerdface," she said.

Brother laughed nervously. "Well, we gotta go," he said.

"That's right," said Bermuda. "Brother's walking me home."

Sister was still glaring at Brother. "But the McBears live on the other side of town," she said. "It'll take you over an hour to get home."

"Longer," said Bermuda. "We're stopping at the Burger Bear for shakes, too."

Sister ignored Bermuda and kept her eyes on Brother. "But you'll be home in time for dinner, won't you?"

Bermuda laughed. "You sound more like his *mother* than his sister," she said.

"Butt out!" said Sister.

"Cool it, Sis," said Brother.

"I'm just trying to help you," said Sister.

"I don't need any help!" Brother snapped.

"Oh, yeah? Maybe we should take a vote on that!" Sister shot back.

"Well," said Bermuda, "Brother and I vote for the Burger Bear, and our votes are the only ones that count. Say good-bye, Brother."

"Er, uh...see you later, guys," said Brother sheepishly.

The cubs watched in amazement as Brother and Bermuda walked off down the street hand in hand.

Cousin Fred was still red-faced. But now it was because Bermuda had made fun of him. "I don't like that new girl," he muttered.

"Oh, really?" sneered Sister. "You could have fooled me."

Chapter 7
Brother in Trouble?

For a while, as the cubs made their way home, Sister and Fred were too embarrassed to say anything to Bonnie. They both hated the way Brother was treating her. And they weren't too happy about the way he'd treated *them,* either.

Finally Sister spoke up. "What's gotten into that brother of mine?" she said. "His new 'friend' was mean to all three of us, and he just stood there and watched."

"At least he seemed a little embarrassed," said Fred.

"Embarrassed doesn't cut it," said Sister angrily. "Did you hear that crack she made about my acting like his mother? And she had the nerve to call you—"

"Don't say it!" Fred warned. More than anything else he hated being called a nerd.

BUT I'M NOT JEALOUS.

"And did you see the way she smiled at Bonnie?" Sister went on. "That was no friendly smile. That was an *oh-what-fun-it-is-to-make-you-jealous* smile."

"But I'm not jealous," said Bonnie.

"It's okay, Bonnie," said Sister. "You can admit it to us. We're your friends."

"No, really," said Bonnie. "I'll admit I *was* jealous. Well, maybe I still am, a little. But now I'm mostly worried about Brother."

At first Sister and Fred didn't believe Bonnie. But it was true. Something funny had happened deep inside Bonnie's heart. When Brother had appeared holding hands with Bermuda, she'd been jealous—*very* jealous. But after watching Brother stand by without a word of protest as Bermuda insulted his own sister and his best buddy, Bonnie had had another change of heart. The jealousy had nearly vanished. Instead, she was just embarrassed for Brother. *And* worried about him.

Brother had always been a good cub, a friendly cub—one who cared about other cubs' feelings. Whenever he saw his friends and family insulted or mistreated, he would stand up for them. He even stood up for strangers. But now he seemed to be under some sort of spell. A spell cast by Bermuda McBear.

"After all," Bonnie continued, "I may not be Brother's girlfriend, but I *am* his *friend.* And that's why I'm more worried than jealous."

"*He's* sure not worried about *us,*" grumbled Fred.

"That's exactly what worries me," said Bonnie.

Chapter 8
News from the Gossip Queen

Bonnie Brown's parents were actors who had to travel a lot, so she was living with her aunt and uncle, Lady and Squire Grizzly. When she got back to Grizzly Mansion that afternoon, all she did until dinner was wander from room to room in the vast house, thinking about Brother.

Brother was a good cub who occasionally got into trouble because of other cubs he started hanging out with. Bonnie remembered when he had gotten into trouble by helping the Too-Tall gang pester a substitute teacher at school. And there was the time he had gotten into trouble as editor of a student newspaper because of a mixed-up article Queenie had written about Teacher Bob.

Bonnie had a hunch that Brother was heading for trouble again because of his crush on Bermuda McBear. She knew it was only natural for a shy guy like Brother to get a crush on a good-looking older girl who seemed to like him. But there was something odd about the way Bermuda had come after Brother. Somehow it reminded Bonnie of a shark attacking its prey. Had Bermuda chosen Brother to be her boyfriend because she really liked him so much? Or was there another reason?

Afternoon turned into evening, but Bonnie couldn't stop thinking about Brother

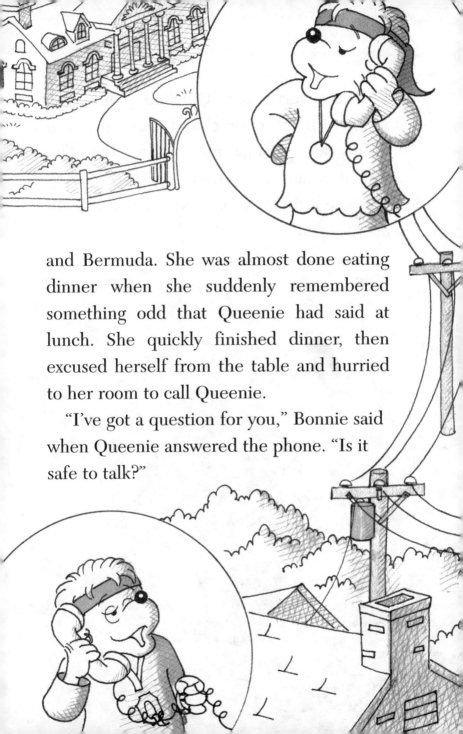

and Bermuda. She was almost done eating dinner when she suddenly remembered something odd that Queenie had said at lunch. She quickly finished dinner, then excused herself from the table and hurried to her room to call Queenie.

"I've got a question for you," Bonnie said when Queenie answered the phone. "Is it safe to talk?"

"Don't worry," said Queenie. "I'm in my room with the door closed, talking to you on my own personal phone line. There's no way Bermuda can listen in. Besides, she's not even here. Get this: she's out with *another guy!*"

"She *is?*" said Bonnie. "Who?"

"Some guy named Cool," said Queenie.

"That's what she called him on the phone. I've got my own special high-tech listening device: it's called 'ear to the wall.' Anyway, I bet he's that Carl King from Miss Glitch's class. The one with the cool black leather jacket and the cool black leather boots. His nickname is Cool."

"Cool Carl King?" said Bonnie. "That's quite a name."

"Betcha can't say it three times fast," said Queenie.

"I won't even try," said Bonnie. "How do you know him?"

"He's a friend of Too-Tall's," said Queenie. "He's the same age as Too-Tall. Too-Tall would be in Miss Glitch's class, too, if he hadn't been kept back twice."

"That makes Cool a year older than Bermuda," said Bonnie.

"Right," said Queenie. "This girl's some-

thin' else, isn't she? She's got a boyfriend a year older than her, and another one a year younger. I guess she doesn't go for guys her own age. Anyway, she ran out a few minutes ago to meet Cool at the Burger Bear. Can you believe that? She takes Brother there before dinner, then meets another guy there *after* dinner!"

"This is awful," said Bonnie. "Brother would be crushed if he knew."

"It gets worse," said Queenie. "After talking to Cool, Bermuda called Brother and got him to invite her to go along with him on his rounds as principal's aide tomorrow. Then she told him she couldn't walk home with him after school. She said she has to wait at school for my mom to pick her up to take her shopping."

"Is that true?" asked Bonnie.

"Fat chance," said Queenie. "She's probably meeting Cool somewhere instead. Bonnie, you've got nothing to worry about. Something tells me Brother's gonna come running back to you any day now. By the way, what was the question you wanted to ask me?"

"I almost forgot," said Bonnie. "When you saw Bermuda with Brother at lunch, you said, 'I guess it was just a matter of time.' Did Bermuda have her eye on Brother before today?"

"Well, sort of," said Queenie. "Yesterday she asked me who the principal's aide was this month. I told her it was Brother Bear. One of her classmates must have pointed him out to her in the lunchroom."

"Hmm," said Bonnie. "That girl is obviously up to something."

"Like what?" asked Queenie.

"I don't know yet," said Bonnie. "But I just thought of a way to find out...Thanks, Queenie. Gotta go."

HMM. THAT GIRL IS OBVIOUSLY UP TO SOMETHING.

Chapter 9
Let's Do Lunch

Bonnie put her new plan into action the very next morning. She gathered Sister Bear, Cousin Fred, and Lizzy Bruin together in the schoolyard before the morning bell.

"We've got to do something to help Brother," she said. "And I've got an idea."

"I'm not speaking to Brother," Sister grumped.

"Me, neither," said Lizzy. Cousin Fred nodded in agreement.

"You don't have to talk to him," said Bonnie. "There's not enough time to explain now. Can you meet me at lunch?"

Sister and Fred glanced at each other. "Okay," said Sister. "I guess we can do that much."

"I'll bring my brother Barry," said Lizzy. "Maybe he can help."

"Don't," said Bonnie.

"Why not?" asked Lizzy.

"He's not a Bear Detective," said Bonnie.

Lizzy, Sister, and Fred looked at one another, then at Bonnie.

"You want the Bear Detectives to investigate?" said Fred. "Without Brother?"

"I could take Brother's place for now," suggested Bonnie. "You guys can teach me how to be a Bear Detective."

"I don't know," said Fred. "We've never investigated one of our own members before."

"But we won't be investigating Brother," said Bonnie. "We'll be investigating Bermuda McBear."

"Hmm," said Fred. He turned to Sister and Lizzy. They whispered among themselves.

"All right," said Fred, turning back to Bonnie. "We'll listen to your idea. But why meet at lunch? Why not wait until after school?"

"By then it'll be too late," said Bonnie. "I'll explain everything at lunch."

47

Chapter 10
Triangles

Bonnie and the Bear Detectives weren't the only cubs talking about Brother and Bermuda that morning. All across the schoolyard, cubs whispered, pointed, giggled, and winked at each other.

The two lovebirds were off by themselves holding hands. At first no one bothered them. But that changed the moment Too-Tall and his gang arrived.

"Well, well!" boomed Too-Tall as he came through the front gate. "If it isn't *Romeo and Juliet!*" Then, with his head thrown back and arms outstretched, he strutted right past Brother and Bermuda, crooning, "*Romeo, Romeo...wherefore art thou, Romeo?*" Skuzz, Smirk, and Vinnie made kissing noises in the background.

Meanwhile, a group of cubs had collected around Ferdy Factual and Trudy Brunowitz. "What we have here is a triangle," Ferdy was lecturing, "with Brother Bear, Bonnie Brown, and Bermuda McBear as the three sides. Now, there are different kinds of triangles. Some are *equilateral,* with the sides equal in length. Others are *isosceles,* in which only two of the sides are equal. I don't know whether our present triangle is isosceles, since I'm not sure whether Bonnie and Bermuda are equal. But it is certainly not equilateral, because Brother is *clearly* unequal to either Bonnie or Bermuda."

Ferdy threw his head back and laughed. Trudy laughed politely, but none of the other cubs did.

"What's the matter with the rest of you?" said Ferdy. "Was that joke too clever for you?"

With a sneaky smile on his face, Barry Bruin said, "I don't think our triangle is equilateral *or* iso-isos—whatever you said."

"You don't?" said Ferdy. "Then what kind of a triangle is it?"

"It's...the *Bermuda Triangle!*" cried Barry. "Ha! Ha! Ha!"

Ferdy rolled his eyes, but Trudy Brunowitz and Harry McGill laughed as hard as Barry.

"I don't get it," said Gil Grizzwold.

"It's a pun," said Trudy, still giggling. "Near the island of Bermuda is a patch of sea called the Bermuda Triangle, where ships have mysteriously disappeared and never been heard from again." She jabbed

Ferdy in the ribs with her elbow. "Come on, Ferd, admit it. It's funny."

Ferdy yawned again. "Oh, all right," he said. "I suppose it was pretty good."

"Pretty good?" said Babs. "It was awesome!" But she looked worried instead of amused.

"Is that so?" said Ferdy. "If it was so *awesome*, then why didn't you laugh?"

Babs stared off across the schoolyard at Brother and Bermuda. "Because," she said, "Brother is mysteriously disappearing into our Bermuda Triangle...and we may never hear from him again..."

Chapter 11
Bonnie Makes Her Case

At lunch, Bonnie and the Bear Detectives chose a corner table across the room from where Brother and Bermuda sat gazing into each other's eyes.

"All right, Bonnie," said Cousin Fred. "The first thing we have to do is decide whether or not to take the case. Why should we investigate Bermuda McBear?"

Bonnie told the Bear Detectives about Bermuda meeting Cool at the Burger Bear the night before.

"That stinks!" said Lizzy.

"Sure, it stinks," said Sister. "But all it means is that Bermuda is a rotten two-timer. What's there to investigate?"

"I'm getting to that," said Bonnie. "Two days ago Bermuda asked Queenie who this month's principal's aide is. And yesterday she was all over Brother."

"You mean she's only interested in Brother because he's the principal's aide?" said Sister.

"Exactly," said Bonnie. "And Brother is taking her along on his rounds this afternoon."

"Hmm," said Fred. "That sounds pretty suspicious. I wonder what she's after?"

"Well, let's try to figure it out," said Bonnie. "What does the principal's aide have that other cubs don't?"

The cubs thought as they ate lunch. After a while, Lizzy said, "Brother has the principal's aide badge he got from Mr. Honeycomb."

"Oh, right," said Sister. "Bermuda's after

his badge. Get serious, Lizzy."

"I've got it!" said Bonnie. "Brother has a key to the supply room!"

"Hey, you're right!" said Sister. "I'll bet Bermuda's planning to rob the supply room!"

"And maybe split the loot with that older boyfriend of hers!" added Lizzy.

"Hold your horses," said Fred. "How would Bermuda get the key away from Brother?"

"She doesn't have to!" said Sister. "Brother will let her into the supply room this afternoon when he makes his rounds!"

"How is she going to rob the supply room right in front of Brother?" asked Fred.

At first Sister didn't have an answer. But as she pondered the question, her eyes grew wide. "You don't suppose...," she said, "...that Bermuda...*and Brother*..."

The lunchroom noise was all around them, but Bonnie and the Bear Detectives were silent. Sister hadn't finished her sentence. But she didn't have to.

Can it be? thought Bonnie. *Brother...a burglar?*

All of a sudden Bonnie had a vision of Brother and Bermuda in the supply room, greedily stuffing their backpacks with paper, rulers, pens, pencils, and boxes of staples. Then she frowned. It just didn't make sense. It was true that Brother had been in trouble before. But pestering a substitute teacher was one thing. Burglary was another.

"No way," Bonnie said. "The biggest crush of his life couldn't get Brother to commit burglary. Besides, I forgot to tell you that Bermuda called him last night and told him she couldn't walk home with him after school. She gave him some phony story about going shopping with Mrs. McBear. That hardly sounds like two cubs plotting a burglary."

The Bear Detectives agreed. And they agreed to take the case.

"Great!" said Bonnie. "I think we should start the investigation by following Bermuda after school. That's why we had to meet now."

"Good thinking," said Lizzy. "But we don't call that *'following.'* We call it *'tailing the suspect.'* "

"Got it," said Bonnie.

"When the last bell rings," said Fred, "we'll all get to the front entrance before Bermuda. Once she's out of the building, we'll tail her. Well, I guess that ends our meeting."

"Aren't you forgetting something?" said Sister.

"What's that?" asked Fred.

"Bonnie may only be a temporary member," said Sister, "but she still has to take the secret Bear Detective Oath." Sister looked around to make sure they weren't being watched. "Okay, Bonnie, raise your right hand. Now, repeat after me: I, Bonnie Brown, do solemnly swear to work my hardest to solve every case."

"That's all?" said Bonnie.

"Well, we're not making you president of Bear Country, you know," said Sister. "Hurry up. The bell's gonna ring any second."

And the bell ending lunch did ring just moments after Bonnie finished repeating the Bear Detective Oath.

I, BONNIE BROWN, DO SOLEMNLY SWEAR TO WORK MY HARDEST TO SOLVE EVERY CASE.

Chapter 12
Tailing the Suspect

After school Brother Bear walked home alone. When he passed the Bear Detectives just outside the front entrance, he tried to make eye contact with them. Only Bonnie smiled at him. Sister, Lizzy, and Fred all looked away.

As soon as Brother disappeared down the street, Bermuda came out the entrance and down the front steps so quickly that she didn't even notice the Bear Detectives. She seemed in a real hurry to get somewhere.

The Bear Detectives followed at a safe distance as Bermuda walked through downtown Beartown.

"She's not going home," said Fred. "She would have turned on Beeline Avenue."

"Maybe she's headed for Cool's house," said Lizzy. "To split the loot with him."

"What loot?" said Sister.

"The loot from the supply room, of course," said Lizzy.

"But her backpack isn't even half full," said Sister. "Get real, Lizzy."

Soon the cubs realized that Bermuda wasn't headed for Cool's house. In the heart of the shopping district, she stopped in front of Beartown's big computer store, Bearware.

"Look," said Fred. "She's going in. Maybe she really *is* going shopping."

"Then where's Mrs. McBear?" asked Sister.

"I don't know," said Fred. "Inside, maybe. Wait a minute. I just thought of something.

The supply room at school connects with the computer room. The main doors to both rooms are always locked, but the connecting door is always open. Too-Tall told me."

"How does he know that?" asked Lizzy.

"Too-Tall knows everything," said Sister. "What are you getting at, Fred?"

"If Too-Tall knows, Cool probably knows, too," said Fred. "He could have told Bermuda. Maybe she stole something from the computer room while Brother was in the supply room."

"Like what?" said Sister. "A computer? That wouldn't even fit in her backpack!"

"Hey, we're wasting time," said Bonnie. "Let's go after her."

"But if we go in, she might see us," said Fred.

"We'll just have to take that chance," said Bonnie.

A bell went *ding dong* as the Bear Detectives opened Bearware's front door and slipped inside. Fortunately, Bermuda didn't look up. She was standing in a far corner of the store talking with someone. It was an older boy cub wearing a black leather jacket.

"I bet that's Cool," whispered Bonnie as the cubs hid behind a display case of new software.

"It's Cool Carl," said Fred. "I'd know that jacket anywhere."

"Bingo," said Sister. "The older boy-friend."

"Look," said Lizzy. "She's taking something out of her backpack."

It was an ordinary notepad. Bermuda tore off the top page and handed it to Cool, who slipped it into one of his jacket pockets. Cool winked at Bermuda and smiled. Then he took her by the hand and led her out of the store.

The Bear Detectives reached the door in time to see Cool and Bermuda split up and walk off in opposite directions.

"Which one do we tail?" asked Sister.

"I don't know," said Fred.

"Maybe we should split up and tail them both," suggested Bonnie.

But by the time the cubs had decided to stick with Bermuda, she had already turned a corner and disappeared from sight.

Chapter 13
"Elementary, My Dear Lizzy"

Lizzy shook her head and sighed as the Bear Detectives walked home from Bearware.

"Don't be discouraged, Liz," said Sister. "We did our best to keep up with Bermuda."

"It's not that," said Lizzy. "We went to all this trouble to investigate her, and it turns out that all she stole was one crummy notepad!"

The others laughed.

"That sounds like the kind of thing your brother would say," Fred teased. "Bermuda didn't steal that notepad. But she might have stolen what she wrote on it."

"I'll bet it's information from the school computer system," said Bonnie.

"If you're right," said Fred, "then Bermuda's a hacker."

"What's a hacker?" asked Sister.

"Hackers break into computer systems they don't belong in," Fred explained. "Sometimes they steal private information from the files. And sometimes they mess up the files or the computer programs."

"Well, whatever it was she stole, it couldn't have been much," said Sister. "That notepad has pretty small pages."

"What do you think it was?" asked Lizzy.

"Beats me," said Sister. "What kind of stuff is on the school computer system, anyway?"

"Who knows?" said Fred. "It's all secret. Only Mr. Honeycomb, Mr. Grizzmeyer, and the teachers can get into it. It's completely separate from the computers we use in class."

"The only way to find out what she stole," said Bonnie, "is to get our hands on that piece of paper she gave to Carl. But how?"

"Maybe we could get Too-Tall to steal it from him," suggested Sister.

"Nah," said Fred. "Too-Tall and Cool are good buddies. Too-Tall may be a great big jerk to the rest of us most of the time, but he'd never double-cross a close friend."

Sister shook her head sadly. "Well, that's the end of our investigation," she said. "I guess we'll never know what's on that piece of paper."

The cubs walked along in silence for a time.

Suddenly Fred stopped. "I've got it!" he said. "We don't even need that piece of paper!"

"Oh, sure," Sister scoffed. "I suppose you just bought a great second-hand crystal ball at some garage sale."

But Fred wouldn't be discouraged by snide comments. Quickly he took a pencil and notepad from his backpack. Then he printed his name on it and tore the page off.

"*That's* what you think Bermuda wrote on her notepad?" said Lizzy. "*Cousin Fred?*"

"Gimme a break, Lizzy," said Fred. "I'm not done yet. Now watch this."

Fred rubbed the side of the pencil lead back and forth across the next page of the notepad. "There!" he cried. He held up the notepad for the others to see.

"Wow!" said Bonnie.

"Cool!" said Sister.

The pencil lead had blackened everything across the middle of the page *except* the imprint made by Fred's printing on the page above. In clear white letters in the center of the black patch were the words "Cousin Fred."

"Fred, you're a genius!" said Lizzy.

"Elementary, my dear Lizzy," said Fred. "I saw it in a Bearlock Holmes movie."

"That's great," said Bonnie. "But it means we still have to get ahold of Bermuda's notepad to find out what information she gave Cool."

"True enough," said Fred. "But that's going to be a lot easier than stealing the note from Cool. I just happened to notice yesterday that Bermuda brings her backpack to lunch instead of leaving it in her locker. She hangs it from the back of her chair by one of the shoulder straps."

"But how will we get into it?" asked Lizzy.

"I bet I could crawl over to it and get the notepad without Bermuda or Brother seeing me," said Sister.

"But everyone else in the lunchroom will

notice you crawling across the floor," said Fred. "Bermuda and Brother will see them staring at you."

The cubs thought hard. Finally Bonnie said, "I have it. I can create a diversion while Sister steals the notepad."

"What's a diversion?" asked Sister.

"Diversion," said Fred. *"A distraction intended to draw attention from the point of main attack."*

"What kind of a diversion would you create?" asked Sister.

"I've got until lunchtime tomorrow to figure that out," said Bonnie. "But I can promise you that whatever it is, I'll have every eye in the lunchroom glued to me."

"Are you sure you can be that convincing?" asked Lizzy.

Bonnie chuckled. "Don't forget," she said with a wink. "I'm an actor."

Chapter 14
Bonnie's Bag of Tricks

The next day at lunch, the Bear Detectives took a corner table as usual and waited for the other tables to fill up. As soon as everyone was busy eating and chatting, Sister nodded to Bonnie.

Bonnie had brought her lunch from home in a brown paper bag. When Sister nodded to her, she let out a piercing shriek and jumped up on her chair. "There's something in my lunch bag!" she squealed, pointing down at the table.

At the sound of Bonnie's shriek, all the cubs in the room had turned to look in her direction. Now, as Fred grabbed Bonnie's lunch bag and shook it, they all stood up to watch. Many climbed up on their chairs and craned their necks to get a better look. That's exactly what Bermuda and Brother did as Sister crouched down and made her way toward them through the crowd.

Out of the brown paper bag came a peanut butter and jelly sandwich, followed by a Galaxy candy bar, followed by a long thin scaly thing.

"A *snake!*" shrieked Bonnie.

Nearly everyone in the room screamed at the top of their lungs. Of course, the Bear Detectives were only pretending to be scared. They knew the snake was only a rubber one that Bonnie had bought at Beartown Theatrical Supply.

Meanwhile, Sister had reached Bermuda's backpack. Quicker than you can say "Bear Detectives," she stuck her hand into the backpack and pulled out the notepad.

As Sister headed back toward the Bear

Detectives' table, Fred pretended to discover that the snake was a fake. "It's a practical joke!" he told Bonnie.

At that, a wave of laughter swept through the room. Of course, no one laughed harder than Too-Tall and his gang.

Bonnie scowled and pointed a finger at Too-Tall. "It was you!" she cried. "You did this! How in the world did you get that thing into my lunch bag?"

At first Too-Tall looked shocked at Bonnie's accusation. Then a smile came to his face as he folded his arms across his chest. "That's for me to know and you to find out," he said proudly.

There were shouts of "Great gag, Too-Tall!" and "Way to go, big guy!" from the other cubs. Too-Tall beamed as Miss Glitch, the teacher on lunchroom duty, stood over him with an angry frown on her face.

"You ought to be ashamed of yourself,
young man!" said Miss Glitch. "Another
black mark for bad behavior will go on your
school record!"

Too-Tall just shrugged and doffed his cap.
The other cubs roared with laughter.

Sister slipped back into her seat at the
Bear Detectives' table. "Poor Too-Tall," she

said. "I didn't know we were going to get him in trouble."

"But I had to be convincing," said Bonnie. "Who would *you* have accused of putting a rubber snake in your lunch bag? Ferdy Factual? Besides, you saw what happened. The big jerk pretended he did it so he could take credit for a great practical joke in front of his fans."

"But he got another black mark...," said Sister.

"Too-Tall *likes* black marks," said Fred. "What about the notebook? Didn't you get it?"

"It's under my seat," said Sister.

Fred looked under Sister's chair. "Where?"

"I mean the seat that's attached to the rest of my body," said Sister. "I'm sitting on it."

"Give it here," said Fred. "Nobody's watching anymore."

Quickly Fred took out a pencil and rubbed the lead across the top page of the notepad while the others leaned across the table to watch. Something was becoming visible on the page...

" '555-3500,' " Fred read. "Maybe it's some kind of secret code."

"Like a computer password?" asked Sister.

"Maybe," said Fred.

Sister groaned. "Then we'll *never* figure out what it means," she said glumly.

"Wait a minute," said Bonnie. "It looks like a phone number."

"Yes, it does!" said Lizzy.

"It must be a local number," said Fred. "There's no area code."

"Great," moaned Sister. "We're all worried about Bermuda hacking the school computer system, and all she gives to Cool is some dumb phone number!"

"I still think she's a hacker," said Fred. "She probably used this notepad again after giving Cool the note. The phone number must be the imprint from a different page."

"Well, that does it," said Sister. "We're sunk."

"Now, come on, guys," said Bonnie. "We're Bear Detectives, remember? We've sworn to work our hardest to solve every case. The least we can do is call this number and see what happens."

Chapter 15
Hacking for a Good Cause

Unfortunately, the Bear Detectives were in for another disappointment. When they used the pay phone on the corner after school to call the number on the notepad, all they heard was a bunch of weird beeps and squeals.

"The number must have been disconnected," said Bonnie, hanging up the phone.

"Why would Bermuda give Cool a disconnected number?" asked Sister.

"Beats me," said Bonnie.

"I guess she's not a hacker, after all," said Lizzy.

"I still think she stole something from that computer room," said Bonnie. "Maybe the phone number has nothing to do with it."

"So what do we now?" asked Sister.

The cubs leaned against the phone booth, thinking.

At last, Fred said, "I've only got one idea left. Harry McGill. He knows as much about computers as any cub in Beartown. Maybe he can think of something."

"It's worth a try," said Bonnie. "Let's go see if he's home."

The cubs hurried to Harry's house and rang the doorbell. Mrs. McGill answered the door and told them that Harry was in his room. The cubs tramped upstairs and found the door to Harry's room open.

"Hi, guys," said Harry, looking up from his computer. "Come on in. What's up?"

"We need some advice," said Bonnie. "About an unsolved Bear Detectives case."

"That sounds a lot more interesting than this computer game I'm playing," said Harry. "I'm all ears."

Bonnie told him the whole story from start to finish.

"Hmm," said Harry. "Bermuda McBear a hacker? Seems more likely that if there's a

hacker mixed up in this, it's Cool Carl King. He's a real computer whiz. Too-Tall took me over to his house a couple of weeks ago before one of our weekly chess matches. He's got a computer with all the newest gadgets, a high-speed printer, and a bookcase full of software."

"A computer whiz," said Bonnie, thinking. "That must be why Bermuda met him at Bearware. But all she gave him was this disconnected phone number." She handed Bermuda's notepad to Harry.

Harry looked at the phone number and frowned. "Disconnected?" he said. "What did you hear when you called it?"

"A bunch of funny beeps and squeals," said Bonnie.

Something made Harry smile. "That's not what you hear when a number's been disconnected," he said. "You hear a recorded message saying it's been disconnected."

"My gosh, that's right," said Fred. "Why didn't we think of that?"

"Well, *something's* wrong with the number," said Sister.

"I bet there's nothing wrong with this number," said Harry, still smiling. "You just called it from the wrong kind of phone."

"Wrong kind of phone?" said Lizzy. "What's the *right* kind of phone?"

"One with a modem," said Harry.

"What's a modem?" asked Lizzy.

Harry swiveled his wheelchair so he could reach a piece of equipment on his computer desk. He patted it and said, "This, my friends, is a modem. It's connected to my computer's phone."

"Computers have phones?" said Sister.

"They do if their owners want to communicate with other computers," said Harry.

"Who would want to communicate with Bear Country School's computer?" asked Lizzy.

"Other schools, teachers with home computers," said Harry. "And, apparently, Cool Carl King. Now watch this."

Harry opened another program and typed in the number on Bermuda's notepad. Within seconds, a message flashed onto the screen. In large letters it said: WELCOME TO BEAR COUNTRY SCHOOL. Then, below that, in smaller letters, it said: *Please type your name.*

"There!" said Harry. "That proves it. Cool

Carl wanted to hack the school computer system from his home computer. To do it, he needed the system's secret phone number. And he knew that a computer's phone number is usually taped to all the modems in the system."

"So he got his girlfriend to pretend to like Brother," said Fred, "because he knew that Brother has a key to the supply room, which connects to the computer room through an unlocked door."

"Exactly!" said Bonnie. "And once Brother let Bermuda into the supply room, all she had to do was slip into the computer room while Brother was checking supplies, find a modem, and jot down the number!"

"Bingo!" cried Sister. "Case solved!"

"Not so fast," said Bonnie. "We figured out what Bermuda stole. But Cool's the real hacker. And we still don't know what *he*

stole from the school computer."

Fred nodded at the computer screen. "Now's our chance to find out," he said. "Let's check out the school's computer files."

"Yeah!" said Lizzy. "Go ahead, Harry. Type in your name, like it says!"

The other cubs laughed.

"There aren't any files under *my* name,"

said Harry. "Most of them must be under the names of teachers."

"Cool Carl is in Miss Glitch's class," said Fred. "Maybe he stole something from her files."

Harry typed in *Miss Glitch*. Moments later, a list of four items appeared on the screen.

Harry read them aloud. "MH.doc, SH.doc, HH.doc, and HT.doc."

"Computer mumbo jumbo," muttered Sister.

"No sweat," said Harry. "They're file codes. *Doc* stands for 'document.' And each pair of letters probably stands for something in one of the files. Let's see if I'm right."

The Bear Detectives crowded round as Harry typed in the first three file codes one by one. And he was right. MH stood for "Math Homework." SH stood for "Science

Homework." And HH stood for "History Homework."

"I can't imagine what Cool Carl would want with homework assignments," said Fred.

"There's still one file left," said Bonnie. "That *has* to be it."

Harry pressed a few more keys. The last file appeared on the screen.

The cubs let out a gasp all at once.

"*Double* bingo!" cried Sister.

Across the top of the screen were the

words HISTORY TEST. Below them was a series of questions about the history of Bear Country.

"Cool must have looked at this test when he hacked the system," said Harry. "Maybe he even made a copy of it with his printer."

"Hey!" said Bonnie. "Turn it off, Harry! We're breaking into a private computer! That makes *us* hackers, too!"

"But we're hacking for a good cause," said Fred.

"We're finished, anyway," said Harry. He cleared the screen and switched off the computer.

"We should make Harry an honorary Bear Detective," Fred told his partners. "We never could have solved the case without him."

"There's still one problem," said Bonnie. "We may have solved the case, but how can

we prove that Cool actually called the school computer?"

"No sweat," said Harry. "The phone company keeps a record of all calls made."

"Great!" said Bonnie. But then she put a hand to her mouth. "Uh-oh! Then the phone company will have a record of the call *we* just made, too!"

Harry picked up his regular phone and handed it to Bonnie. "You'd better call the school right away and explain everything to Mr. Honeycomb," he said. "He's the one who should contact the phone company, anyway."

Chapter 16
Bermuda's Confession

Luckily, Mr. Honeycomb was still in his office when Bonnie called. He listened carefully to everything she told him, then called Miss Glitch into the office. Soon after talking with Miss Glitch, he called the Bears' tree house and the McBear home and asked Bermuda and Brother to come back to school right away, along with Mrs. McBear and Mama and Papa Bear. The Bear Detectives went back to school, too, and waited for Brother on the front steps. Queenie also came along with Bermuda.

It was a long time before Brother finally appeared. He looked exhausted. Mama and Papa waited for him in the family car while he talked to his friends.

"I don't know what to say, guys," he said, "except that I'm really glad you solved this case. And I'm really sorry for everything."

Bonnie was the first to speak up. "We forgive you," she said. "Getting a crush on someone can make a bear do some pretty silly things."

"It was awful watching Bermuda wrap you around her little finger like that," said Queenie.

Brother looked surprised. "Awful?" he said. "That's exactly how you treat Too-Tall. What's the difference?"

Queenie smiled. "The difference is you're

not a great big jerk most of the time."

When everyone finished laughing at that, they felt a little more relaxed.

"What's your punishment?" asked Queenie.

"I got one black mark for letting Bermuda into the supply room," said Brother.

"Piece o' cake," said Sister. "What about Bermuda?"

"She got suspended for three days," said Brother.

"Is that all?" gasped Sister. "After what she did?"

"I think I understand why Mr. Honeycomb decided to go easy on her," said Brother. "She cried through the whole meeting. She talked about how she missed her friends and family and couldn't seem to make any new friends here by being nice. Maybe that's why she turned nasty. The

instant Cool was nice to her, she got a huge crush on him. Then he threatened to stop dating her if she didn't help him hack the school computer. She was under a lot of pressure."

"Hey!" said Sister. "You don't even sound mad at her!"

"Oh, I'm still mad at her," said Brother. "But I sort of understand, too. Sometimes older cubs can get you to do things you wouldn't ordinarily do. Especially when you have a crush on them. Believe me, I know. Anyway, Bermuda apologized to me and promised to apologize to all of you, too."

"So where is she?" asked Sister.

"She won't come out until we leave," said Brother. "She's too embarrassed to face you guys right away. She'll call each of you tonight."

"What about Cool?" asked Bonnie. "Why isn't he here?"

"Miss Glitch asked Mr. Honeycomb not to tell him he'd been caught yet," said Brother. "Cool didn't just steal the history test, you know. Bermuda says he printed a bunch of copies and sold them to class-mates. He needed money because he's so hooked on computer games that he already spent his whole allowance for the month. Anyway, the history test is tomorrow morn-

ing, so Miss Glitch is going to spend all evening making up a new test. She said she wants to see Cool's face tomorrow morning when he realizes he's been caught. So don't spread any of this around until lunchtime tomorrow. Especially you, Queenie."

"Me?" said Queenie, pretending to look shocked. "Spread gossip? I wouldn't even think of it!"

"You gotta promise me," said Brother.

"Why?" said Queenie.

Brother smiled. "Because I already know what Cool's punishment is," he said.

Queenie's eyes grew wide. "You do?" she

said. "You gotta tell me! O-o-o-oo, tell me, tell me, *tell me!*"

"Only if you promise," insisted Brother.

"Oh, all right!" moaned Queenie. "I *promise!*"

Brother motioned the cubs to lean in close to him and lowered his voice. "He's going to be suspended for *three months*," he said. "With extra homework. And all the cubs who bought the test from him are going to get a week."

The cubs were silent as they imagined what a three-month suspension with extra homework would be like. It seemed like forever.

"I'm sure glad I'm not in Cool's shoes," said Fred after a while. "Even though they *are* pretty cool shoes…"

Chapter 17
Crime and Punishment

The next morning, the cubs in Miss Glitch's class were all ready to take their history test. Some of them looked nervous. But quite a few were cool and calm. That's because they had bought copies of the test questions from Cool Carl and memorized their answers before coming to school.

Of course, the coolest and calmest of all was Cool Carl himself. In fact, he was smiling from ear to ear. Not only did he know that he would get a perfect score on the test, but he was also looking forward to playing his new computer games after school. He had quite a thick stack of them waiting at home—thanks to the money he'd raised by selling copies of the test.

"Now, class," said Miss Glitch, "I have an important announcement to make about your history test. It seems that a certain member of this class broke into the school computer system and stole the test questions." She turned and stared straight at Cool Carl.

The smile on Cool's face froze.

"As a result," continued Miss Glitch, "I

had to spend the entire evening last night making up new questions. I expect that those of you who have memorized the answers to the stolen test will flunk the new one. And then we'll know who you are."

By now, Cool's frozen smile had melted completely. He had a lump in his throat the size of a softball. He tried to swallow as Miss Glitch turned to look at him again.

"Oh, yes, Carl," she said. "You will not be taking today's test."

Cool squirmed in his seat. "I...I won't?" he said in a high, squeaky voice.

"No," said Miss Glitch. "In fact, you won't be taking any tests for quite a while."

Cool's face turned as white as a sheet. "Er...uh...why not?" he squeaked.

Miss Glitch smiled. "I suggest you report immediately to Mr. Honeycomb's office," she said. "I'm quite sure he'll be glad to explain everything."

Stan and Jan Berenstain began writing and illustrating books for children in the early 1960s, when their two young sons were beginning to read. That marked the start of the best-selling Berenstain Bears series. Now, with more than one hundred books in print, videos, television shows, and even Berenstain Bears attractions at major amusement parks, it's hard to tell where the Bears end and the Berenstains begin!

Stan and Jan make their home in Bucks County, Pennsylvania, near their sons—Leo, a writer, and Michael, an illustrator—who are helping them with Big Chapter Books stories and pictures. They plan on writing and illustrating many more books for children, especially for their four grand-children, who keep them well in touch with the kids of today.